Crocodile on the Loose!

Harriet and Anthea arrived at the teachers' Staff Room door and peered inside.

Miss Wilson was lying on the sofa . . .

What was left of the sofa. Something had chewed up the cushions and made a start on the foam rubber upholstery.

Mr. Tiger's pipe was lying on the floor, with the stem half broken—but there was no sign of Mr. Tiger.

"It's eaten Mr. Tiger!" cried Anthea.

"Not just Mr. Tiger," said Harriet, looking worried, as she considered the evidence: Mrs. Whitten's half-eaten shoe, Mr. Cousins' chewed coat, Miss Ash's exercise books, and Miss Tremloe's guitar. They were strewn around the floor, with large toothbites in each one.

"What is the meaning of this, Harriet?" said Miss Granston, appearing at the door.

Books by Martin Waddell

Harriet and the Crocodiles
Harriet and the Haunted School

Available from MINSTREL BOOKS

Harriet and the Crocodiles

Martin Waddell

Illustrated by
Mark Burgess

A MINSTREL™ BOOK

PUBLISHED BY
SIMON & SCHUSTER, INC.

A MINSTREL BOOK published by
Simon & Schuster, Inc., 1230 Avenue
of the Americas, New York, New York 10020

Text copyright © 1982, 1984 by Martin Waddell
Illustrations copyright © 1982, 1984 by Mark Burgess
Cover artwork copyright © 1986 by Rob Sauber

Published by arrangement with Little, Brown and Company, Inc.
Library of Congress Catalog Card Number: 83-25530

ISBN: 0-671-61730-3

First Minstrel Books printing August, 1986

10 9 8 7 6 5 4 3 2 1

A MINSTREL BOOK and colophon are trademarks
of Simon & Schuster, Inc.

Printed in the U.S.A.

Contents

A BOOK FOR THE CHILDREN
WHO PLAYED *BUILD A STORY* WITH ME
IN SPRING AND SUMMER 1980
AND
THOSE WHO HAVE YET TO TRY IT!

*The BUILD A STORY technique from which
this book was derived has been developed
by me in association with the "Writers in
Schools" Scheme operated by the Northern
Ireland Arts Council.
In this connection I owe a special debt
to the Northern Ireland Arts Council and
to all the teachers and pupils who have made
this book possible.*

Harriet
and the
Crocodiles

1 | Harriet Rules OK!

"HARRIET!" gasped the Headmistress, going deathly pale. People often did that when they saw Harriet coming, so Harriet didn't take any notice.

"Good morning, Miss Granston," she said, politely removing half her bubble gum from her mouth before she spoke, and sticking it on her schoolbag. Then Harriet bounced on down the corridor, pigtails flying, and kicked open the door of P7.

"OH NO!" groaned Miss Granston, and the Zoo Trip List dropped from her fingers and fluttered to the floor.

Just to make certain it was Harriet, and

not a mirage, Miss Granston crept down the corridor and crouched by the door of P7, squinting through the curtains.

Harriet was sitting on her desk, where she was blowing a huge Harriet-type bubble with the other half of the bubble gum. It burst and stuck to her nose.

"Aaaaaaaah!" screamed Miss Granston, and she fled to the Staff Room.

"What's up?" said Mr. Tiger, when the Headmistress rushed in.

She told him.

Miss Ash went white.

Miss Tremloe trembled.

Mrs. Whitten had one of her dizzy spells, and upset her coffee over her tartan trousers.

"I can't! I won't!" screamed Miss Wilson, who was supposed to be taking P7 to the Zoo. "You told me she wouldn't be here, Headmistress! You lied! You lied!"

"Now, now! We must all keep calm," said Miss Granston weakly. "Harriet is only a child, after all."

"I refuse to take Harriet to the Zoo!"

cried Miss Wilson tearfully. "I won't! I won't! I have my family to consider."

"I wouldn't mind taking Harriet to the Zoo, if I could be sure of leaving her there," remarked Mr. Tiger philosophically. "But I doubt if they have a cage strong enough to hold her."

"Harriet or no Harriet," said Miss Granston, "*someone* is taking P7 to the Zoo."

"No! No! No! No! No! No!" said Miss Wilson, weaving her way to the Staff Toilet.

"Come on, Staff! Play the Game!" snapped Miss Granston. "Show the Slow Street Primary Spirit! Who is going to volunteer to take P7 to the Zoo?"

No hands went up.

Then the Staff Room door opened, and little Mr. Cousins waddled in, in his motorcycling boots. "Morning, everybody," he said cheerfully.

Mr. Cousins was a substitute teacher. It was his first week at Slow Street Primary, where he was filling in for Cecil Watkins.

"Ah, Mr. Cousins," said Miss Granston,

her little piggy eyes gleaming. "I wonder, would you very much mind standing in for Miss Wilson and taking P7 to the Zoo today?"

"Certainly, Headmistress," said Mr. Cousins. He was bald and fat and cheerful, and he liked Zoos and children, and he had never heard of Harriet, who had been out all week with the flu. If he had heard of Harriet, he might have answered differently.

"Well done; that's the Slow Street Spirit," said Miss Granston, and she heaved a sigh of relief and retreated to her office.

"It's only a Zoo Trip, after all!" said Mr. Cousins, innocently puzzled by all the fuss.

"But *you're* doing it!" Miss Tremloe burst out.

"Not *us*!" said Miss Whitten, Miss Ash, and Mrs. Barton, in chorus.

"Jolly good show!" said Mr. Tiger, and he shook Mr. Cousins warmly by the hand.

"Who did it?" demanded Harriet. "Who took my Yellow Snail?"

Nobody owned up.

Harriet loved her snail. It was the world champion of Slow Street School. Now someone had stolen it.

"I'm going to thump *someone*," Harriet muttered fiercely, and she started rolling up the sleeves of her cardigan. Then she removed her bubble gum and stuck it on Anthea, who was her best friend.

"It wasn't me," said Anthea. She was small and wore glasses, and sometimes believed in fairies.

"It was Marky," said Charlie Green.

"It wasn't. It was Charlie," said Marky, retreating behind his desk.

Harriet glowered. She advanced toward them.

"Him! Him!" said Marky despairingly.

"NO! HIM!" cried Charlie.

"It wasn't me," said Sylvester Wise. "And you can't hit me; I've got glasses!" Then he took up a position of safety, crouching behind his desk with his schoolbag over his head.

"OUT OF MY WAY!" roared Harriet.

Small pupils fled.

The floor trembled as Harriet came forward.

THUMP!

THUMP!

AAAAAAAAGGGGGGGUGHHH!

The classroom door opened.

"Good morning, P7! It is your Zoo Day," said little Mr. Cousins, beaming round the room through his big glasses.

Then he stopped, and blinked.

A dazed-looking boy was sitting in the wastepaper basket. Another was hanging by the back of his school jacket from Miss Wilson's coat hook, behind the desk.

"Who did that?" Mr. Cousins gasped.

"Please, Sir!" said Sylvester Wise, wagging his hand eagerly. "Please, Sir! Sir, Sir, please! It was Harriet!"

2 | Harriet Chooses a Bodyguard

Twenty-eight children and a menacing bubble got onto the Slow Street School minibus.

"All present and correct, Headmistress," Mr. Cousins called to Miss Granston, who was crouching behind the milk crates as an elementary anti-Harriet precaution.

"Well done, Mr. Cousins! Oh, well done!" exclaimed Miss Granston, who could scarcely believe her luck.

"Just part of the job," said Mr. Cousins cheerfully, and he climbed into the minibus.

The bus left the school, and Miss Granston went to help the carpenter get Miss Wilson out of the Staff Toilet, where she had locked herself in.

Mr. Cousins sat in the front seat.

Harriet and Anthea sat at the back.

Silent.

Harriet was seldom silent. It was a bad sign. When Harriet was silent, it meant that Harriet was thinking, and after Harriet *thought*, things usually started happening.

Someone had taken Harriet's Yellow Snail. It was the World Champion Snail of Slow Street Primary. Harriet had painted its shell yellow because it was World Champion. She said it was World Champion because it could beat up any other snail in the school. Harriet carried it around with her, as a bodyguard. She had learned a Special Snail Whistle that brought it running when she wanted it . . . running, that is, in snail terms, which means very slowly.

Harriet arrived back in school after being out sick, and whistled: no snail. The Special Sock she kept it in was empty. Someone had removed her snail, without Harriet's permission.

No snail.

And Harriet was going to the Zoo.

Anthea guessed what was on Harriet's mind.

"Are you sure you've looked everywhere for your snail, Harriet?" Anthea asked.

"Everywhere," said Harriet, who had had a busy time snail searching. She had been through all the lunchboxes and most of the pockets, although she had to turn Sylvester Wise upside down to get at his. She had looked in the fish tank in case her snail had drowned, and up and down the map of the world in case he had gone to sleep on a yellow part of the map, where he wouldn't be noticed. No snail.

"What about on the weighing scales?" Anthea suggested. "He might have gone for a swing. You know your snail likes swing-ing."

"He has his own swing at home," said Harriet.

"What about . . . what about in with the

hamster, in his cage?" said Anthea, and then her eyes widened. "The hamster might have *eaten* your snail, Harriet."

"My snail could take on any old hamster, with his stalks tied behind his back," said Harriet. "It's no use, Anthea. I've got to look for something else."

"Not a lion, Harriet," Anthea said, nervously. "I don't like lions. Something ... something nice and *small*, Harriet. I have a goldfish. If you like you could borrow my goldfish."

Harriet blew a mean bubble. She didn't think much of goldfish.

"A white rabbit?" suggested Anthea, hopefully.

"I wouldn't waste my Special Whistle on a *rabbit*," said Harriet scornfully.

The Slow Street minibus arrived at the Zoo, and they all got out.

"Keep together, children," said little Mr. Cousins amiably.

They went to the Monkey House.

Harriet looked at the gorilla.

The gorilla looked at Harriet.

"Oh look," said Charlie Green. "Now there's two of them."

Twenty-eight children and a menacing bubble went into the Monkey House, but only twenty-seven and a menacing bubble came out.

"Twenty-seven?" muttered Mr. Cousins, scratching the hair on his head. It was the only hair he had got, just the one, and he had to be very careful of it, but sometimes he forgot and scratched it. "Twenty-seven? Who is missing?"

"Sir! Sir! Please, Sir! Please! Charlie Green is, Sir!" babbled Sylvester Wise.

"Well I never!" said Mr. Cousins. He stopped scratching his hair, and patted it back into place. "Where can the boy be?"

He went back into the Monkey House.

The large monkey in the third cage from the end looked familiar. It was making funny noises, and dangling upside down by the strap of a schoolbag from the branch of a tree.

"Green? Green? Is that you, Green?" Mr. Cousins said, peering at it closely through the bars. It was either Green or a monkey, and as there wasn't much difference, he couldn't be sure.

"Yussir," said Charlie. Someone had stuffed a squashy banana in his mouth, and it made talking difficult.

"Come out of there at once!" thundered Mr. Cousins. He meant to thunder, but it was more of a high squeak, because he was rather small and had to be careful of his chest.

Then Charlie pointed out that he couldn't come out because he was dangling upside down by the strap of his schoolbag with a large banana stuffed in his mouth. Charlie didn't say it very clearly, because of the banana, but Mr. Cousins got the message.

"I don't know what children are coming to these days," he muttered. Then he demanded, "How on earth did you get like that, boy?" in his sternest voice, which was wheezier than his thundering one, because of the bad chest.

"Sir! Sir! Please, Sir!" shouted Sylvester

Wise, jumping happily up and down. "Sir, Sir! Please, Sir! It was Harriet, Sir!"

"*Come here, Harriet!*" said Mr. Cousins.

But Harriet was nowhere to be seen.

"Not a cobra, Harriet," said Anthea nervously.

"I *like* cobras," said Harriet. "They crush things."

"Little things," said Anthea.

"That's right,"said Harriet.

"Little things *like me*," said Anthea, and she looked as if she was going to cry all over her nice uniform, which was neater and cleaner and greener than anybody else's, because Anthea never did anything to dirty it. Anthea was a very clean, neat, and nice person, but she made up for it by being Best Friends with Harriet.

"Okey-dokey," said Harriet, seeing the tears coming. "No cobras if you don't want them, Anthea."

"I don't," sniffed Anthea.

They wandered out of the Snake House

and inspected the giraffe. Harriet decided it was too big.

"Seal?" said Anthea hopefully, and she pointed out one that would have looked exactly like Mr. Tiger, if it had been smoking a pipe.

"I don't want to look at *him* all day," said Harriet. "I don't know what to do. Life just won't be the same without my snail."

She sat down on a seat and thought about the World Champion, and blew a few mournful gum bubbles.

"I want . . . I want a new Super Pet. Something nobody else in our school would even think of," said Harriet.

"Not creepy-crawlies," insisted Anthea.

"No."

"Not snakes. Not cobras."

"No."

"Not lions or tigers, Harriet."

"There isn't much left," said Harriet moodily.

She blew a big bubble, and then she had an idea. It was a lovely idea. No one else in P7 would have thought of it. It made her

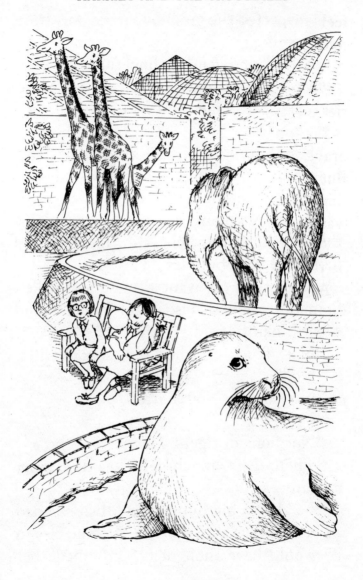

feel proud and happy all over, and so she told Anthea about it.

"Oh," said Anthea.

"What do you mean, 'Oh'?" asked Harriet indignantly.

"I mean 'Oh, how nice,'" said Anthea bravely, though she didn't mean it at all. But she couldn't go on objecting to everything Harriet suggested, because Harriet was her Best Friend.

"Good," said Harriet. "I thought you'd be pleased."

And she went off to get a crocodile.

3 | The Croco-Bus

"We can't take a crocodile on the bus, Harriet," said Anthea anxiously. "The busman won't like it."

"Nonsense," said Harriet, hitching up her wriggling schoolbag.

Harriet's schoolbag didn't usually wriggle. It was wriggling this time because there was a crocodile inside it, eating.

The crocodile was a smallish, friendly crocodile. He had been pottering around his cage looking for another smaller crocodile to eat when Harriet whistled at him.

Harriet's whistle wasn't an ordinary whistle. It was the special Snail Whistle that she used for Training her World Champion. It worked on snails, and it worked on the crocodile.

The crocodile moved toward her as if he was hypnotized. The next thing he knew, he was inside Harriet's schoolbag, nestling up to her lunchbox and eating her notebook. By the time Harriet reached the bus stop, he had eaten her Math book and her pencil case and was making a start on her beret.

"Now we've got it, what do we do with it?" Anthea asked, standing on the side of Harriet which was farthest from the wriggling schoolbag.

"Take it home," said Harriet.

Which is why they were waiting at the bus stop.

"What about the others?" said Anthea. "They'll think we're lost."

Harriet took no notice. She went back to whistling at her crocodile.

Harriet was a good whistler. Her whistle soothed the little crocodile. He stopped wriggling and swallowed the last shreds of the beret. So long as Harriet kept whistling, he was a happy crocodile.

The bus came.

Harriet and Anthea got on, and went to sit in the back.

"There's room beside me," Harriet said, when Anthea made a point of sitting three seats away, just in case.

"I prefer to sit by myself, thank you very much, Harriet," said Anthea, who was worried what might happen next.

"Now then, now then! Stop that whistling!" shouted the conductor toward the back.

Harriet stopped.

Her schoolbag started wriggling.

Harriet started again.

"Stop that whistling! You're annoying the other passengers," the conductor said, advancing down the aisle.

"No I'm not," said Harriet.

"Oh yes, you are," said the conductor, coming to a stop beside her. "This is my bus, and I won't have whistling on it.

Harriet shrugged, and stopped whistling.

The schoolbag gave a gentle wiggle.

The conductor blinked.

"Two tickets, please," said Anthea quickly, thrusting the bus money at him in the hope that she could divert his attention.

"What's that?" said the conductor, pointing at Harriet's wriggling schoolbag. Harriet had taken the schoolbag off when she got on the bus, because the crocodile was rather heavy. Now, with each wriggle, it was inching its way across the seat.

"My schoolbag," said Harriet.

The schoolbag gave a squeak.

Harriet grabbed at the strap, and pursed her mouth to whistle, in the hope that the crocodile would stop wriggling.

"You've got an animal in that!" said the conductor. "No animals allowed on my bus without special permission. I won't have it!"

"You wouldn't *want* it, if you had," said Anthea quietly, but no one heard her.

"Evading fares!" said the conductor, getting quite worked up. "Carrying undeclared animals on a Public Vehicle without paying the appropriate fare is an Offense under Rule 4 subsection 3, of the Public Regulations 1948." He grabbed the wriggling schoolbag, and held it aloft.

"You're caught, you are!" he cried triumphantly. "I call on all my passengers to be witnesses!"

The two men and three boys who were sitting behind them took one look at the schoolbag and one look at Harriet and got off.

"I saw *teeth*," one of them muttered, as he backed away.

"Now then, now then, Miss. I'll have your name and address, if you don't mind," said the conductor. And he put the schoolbag down on the floor, and got out his notebook.

Anthea turned pale.

There was a loud chewing noise coming from the schoolbag. A green snout, edged with sharp teeth, emerged through the side of the bag. It was a leather bag, of the best quality, a Christmas present from Harriet's

Aunt Clemence. The crocodile found it very tasty indeed.

"Name?" said the conductor.

"Harriet," said Harriet.

"H . . . A . . . *Harriet?*" said the conductor, suddenly turning pale.

He put down the pencil and took a closer look at Harriet.

He had seen her somewhere before.

"Not . . . not THE Harriet?" he gurgled.

Harriet's picture, front and side face, was displayed on a Warning Notice with Big Red Letters stuck up on the Public Bus Staff Regulations and Timetables Notice Board.

The bus conductor retreated.

It was the wisest thing to do when confronted by Harriet, but unfortunately he retreated over Harriet's schoolbag, which he had put down on the floor.

Part of Harriet's schoolbag. *Most* of Harriet's schoolbag was already inside the crocodile. He had eaten his way out to look for his Big Green Mom, who had stopped

whistling. He felt lonely, and when he felt lonely, he got hungry.

The crocodile was looking round for something to have a cosy chew at when the bus conductor's trouser leg, complete with sock, shoe, foot, and ankle, presented itself, going backward.

SNAP!

"Aaaaaaaah!" screamed the bus conductor, as he fainted clean away.

"Oh dear," said Harriet.

"I think perhaps we'd better get off the bus, Harriet," said Anthea.

Harriet scooped up her crocodile and stuffed it down inside her cardigan.

Then she got off the bus, whistling softly to keep her crocodile happy.

Miss Granston took the telephone call from Mr. Cousins.

"You've WHAT?" she said. "Say that again!"

A large grin rippled across her face.

"Well done!" she cried. "Oh, well done, Mr. Cousins!"

And she put down the telephone.

Then she did a little hop, skip, and jump of happiness round her room.

It wasn't everyday someone succeeded in Losing Harriet.

"A schoolbag?" said the bemused bus inspector. "You were *bitten* by a SCHOOL-BAG?"

"With big sharp teeth," moaned the conductor, lying back on the seat and clutching his ankle.

"You were bitten by a *schoolbag* with big sharp *teeth?*" said the inspector, slowly.

"Very sharp," said the conductor.

"And this schoolbag bit you?"

"Yes."

"I ... er ... I think you'd better take a holiday. Paid Holiday. Sick Leave. The job's getting too much for you," said the inspector, backing carefully out of range in case anything was catching.

"It was HERS!" the conductor groaned.

"Whose?"

"Harriet's!"

There was a long silence.

"Where is she?" said the inspector, going pale and looking all around him in case Harriet was still there with her man-eating schoolbag. The bus inspector was only two months off retirement age. He wasn't taking any chances.

4 | The Croco-Bath

"Harriet?" said Mr. Smith, politely tapping on the bathroom door. "Harriet dear, are you there?"

No answer.

He tapped a little more loudly, to make himself heard over the whistling and splashing noises.

"HARRIET!"

"Yes, Dad?"

"What are you doing in there, Harriet? Time for supper."

"Yes, Dad. Thanks, Dad. Coming, Dad," said Harriet.

Mr. Smith went downstairs to Mrs. Smith.

"She'll be down in a minute, I expect, dear," he said. "Just playing in the bathroom."

"Not putting cement down the drains again?" Mrs. Smith asked anxiously.

"No, dear."

"Not making custard in the tub?"

"I don't think so, dear," said Mr. Smith.

"Not water bombs?"

"Just playing, dear," said Mr. Smith.

"I hope so," said Mrs. Smith. Then she went into the kitchen and came out with biscuits and bacon and tomato sandwiches, ham rolls, half a chicken and potato salad and ice cream and chocolate fudge for Harriet, to keep her strength up.

CRASH! BANG! CRASH!

Harriet jumped down the staircase and banged through the door, carrying something wrapped up in a well-chewed cardigan.

"A little quieter on the stairs, Harriet dear, could we be, hmmm?" said Mrs. Smith.

"Yes, Mother. Sorry, Mother," said Harriet.

Then she darted over to the fish tank, and slipped something into it, from her cardigan.

"There," she said.

"What's that, dear?" asked Mr. Smith.

"My crocodile," said Harriet.

"How nice, dear," beamed Mrs. Smith.

Harriet ate her biscuits and bacon and tomato sandwiches and ham rolls and chicken and potato salad and ice cream and chocolate fudge and said, "Any seconds?"

"No dear. I'm *terribly* sorry," said Mrs. Smith.

"But I'm hungry," said Harriet.

"And so is your little pet, Harriet," said Mr. Smith, blinking at the fish tank.

"Oh dear," said Mrs. Smith. "Where have all my little fishies gone?"

"I think that Harriet's crocodile has eaten them, dear," said Mr. Smith.

"Must have been feeling peckish, poor little thing," said Mrs. Smith, and she made

a special journey to the kitchen to fetch it some bacon rinds.

SNAP! SNAP!

"Mind your fingers," said Harriet proudly.

"Nippy," said Mr. Smith admiringly.

"Harriet," said little Mrs. Smith. "Harriet, where are you going to keep him, dear?"

"I shall keep him in the bath," said Harriet.

"Oh," said Mrs. Smith.

"Oh, dear me," said Mr. Smith.

"What's the matter?" asked Harriet innocently.

"Well, dear, tomorrow is bath night," said Mr. Smith, looking uneasily at the small crocodile, which was trying to climb out of the fish tank.

"He won't mind sharing," said Harriet.

"My cousin Basil Heartroyd was eaten by a crocodile," said Mr. Smith nervously.

"Not one like Harriet's," said Mrs. Smith.

"Bigger, I should think."

"Much bigger."

"Much."

The two Smiths looked at the crocodile. It was undoubtedly smaller than the crocodile that had eaten Cousin Basil, but its teeth were big. Big *enough*, anyway.

"Very sharp teeth, crocodiles," said Mr. Smith. "There wasn't much of Basil left, you know."

Mrs. Smith looked very upset.

"I don't think I *could* share my bath with your crocodile, Harriet dear," she said. "I'm sorry. I'm just not used to crocodiles."

"I think you'd better find an alternative, Harriet," said Mr. Smith.

"Okay, Dad," said Harriet. "I suppose I can." Then she brightened. "I know," she said. "I'll take him to school with me."

The crocodile grinned.

It may have been a very small crocodile, but it had big ideas.

5 | The Hungry Crocodile

"You're late, Anthea," said Miss Granston. Anthea was so good that she was *never* late, and Miss Granston was very surprised.

"Sorry, Miss Granston," said Anthea.

"Don't let it happen again, Anthea," said Miss Granston, and she stalked off to Assembly.

Anthea opened the cloakroom door.

"Pssst! Harriet! You can come out now. Grannie's gone."

Harriet emerged from the cloakroom, clutching a length of rope, the far end of which was attached to her crocodile.

"Where are you going to put it?" asked Anthea, keeping well out of the way of the gleaming teeth.

"Boiler room," said Harriet, leading the way.

The crocodile waddled down the corridor behind her, looking for something to eat. It tried to tug Harriet sideways to have a nibble at the fire bucket, but, after the first mouthful, decided it didn't like the taste of school sand.

"Come on, Croc," said Harriet, and she whistled softly. The crocodile swished its tail, and waddled on.

Harriet led it to the boiler room, and tied her rope to the boiler.

"Don't worry, Croc," she said, "We'll be in at recess to see you, and we'll bring you our school dinners at dinnertime."

"*You'll* bring it *your* school dinner," said Anthea. She was delicate, and brought lunches. Today's lunch was crab sandwiches and a tomato, which was a special treat. Anthea wasn't giving it to any old crocodile.

"I don't think that is very nice of you, Anthea," said Harriet.

"It's your crocodile," said Anthea. "You feed it."

"I'll let you play with it," said Harriet. "I let you play with my snail, didn't I?"

"Snails aren't crocodiles," said Anthea. "Your snail just sat around all day on a lettuce leaf. It never bit bus conductors, did it?"

"My crocodile was provoked," said Harriet. "Anyway, he was hungry."

"He can go on being hungry," said Anthea. "He's not getting my dinner. I wouldn't mind if it was a school dinner. Nobody likes school dinner. Not even crocodiles."

Harriet thought about school dinners. Soggy peas. Cold potatoes. Spam.

"Maybe there'll be pizza," she said, not very hopefully.

"And maybe there won't," said Anthea, who was a realist. It was Thursday. Pizza was Friday.

They ran down the corridor and barged

into P7, where Miss Wilson got a nasty shock. She had been going around the school singing all morning, because Mr. Cousins had lost Harriet at the Zoo.

"I knew life without Harriet was too good to be true!" she muttered, burying her face in the class register.

Harriet sat down at her desk and yawned. She had been up most of the night whistling to her crocodile, to stop it eating the house. It was a very hungry crocodile. It was the sort of crocodile that might eat *anything*, even school dinners. With that happy thought Harriet set aside the cares and responsibilities of being a crocodile owner, and started bubble blowing again.

Meanwhile, back in the boiler room, the crocodile had chewed its way through the rope, eaten two buckets of coal, and was looking around for something else it could nibble.

At half past ten the bell rang.

Miss Wilson staggered ashen-faced from P7. She had spent an hour and a quarter with Harriet, and emerged almost unscathed, with only a little bubble gum sticking to her pretty fair hair. It was on the curls, just above her forehead.

She made her way slowly up the corridor to the Staff Room, where she was going to tell Miss Granston what she thought of Headmistresses who raised false hopes.

The Staff Room door was closed.

Miss Wilson pushed it open.

She walked in, and collapsed on the sofa beside Mrs. Whitten's crocodile-skin handbag. It wasn't like Mrs. Whitten to leave her handbag behind her, Miss Wilson thought.

Then the handbag opened its mouth.

"Aaaaaaaaah!" screamed Miss Wilson.

SNAP! SNAP!

Harriet, inspecting the chewed rope in the boiler room, heard the scream.

"Oh dear," said Anthea. "Do you think . . ."

"Yes, I do!" said Harriet, and off they sped on a Rescue Mission.

They arrived at the Staff Room door, and peered inside.

Miss Wilson was lying on the sofa.

What was left of the sofa. Something had chewed up the cushions and made a start on the foam rubber upholstery.

It was the same something which had eaten all P6's exercise books, and the wooden table they were piled on, and the three armchairs, and the coats and hats and shoes and the coffeepot and the condensed milk and the kettle and P4's model of Mount Everest.

Mr. Tiger's pipe was lying on the floor, with the stem half broken, and then put to one side, because the tobacco tasted nasty.

Mr. Tiger was most attached to his pipe. Well, usually he was, but now he was unattached. There was the pipe, broken and chewed up on the floor, but there was no sign of Mr. Tiger.

"It's eaten Mr. Tiger!" cried Anthea tearfully. She was upset because she liked Mr. Tiger. He reminded her of her granddad, who was dead. She didn't like to think of him being casually crocodiled.

"Not just Mr. Tiger," said Harriet, looking worried, as she considered the evidence.

41

The evidence was Mrs. Whitten's half-eaten shoe, Mr. Cousins' chewed coat, Miss Ash's exercise books and Miss Tremloe's guitar. They were strewn around the floor, with large toothbites in each one.

"What is the meaning of this, Harriet?" said Miss Granston, appearing at the door.

"Er," said Harriet, "Er, ah, well . . ."

"Please, Miss, Harriet's crocodile has eaten the teachers," said Anthea in a small voice.

"Nonsense," said Miss Granston. "Harriet hasn't got a crocodile!"

"I *have,*" said Harriet indignantly.

"Behave yourself, Harriet," said Miss Granston, sweeping into the room to look for her teachers, just in case.

She tripped over the edge of the rug, and sat down hard on Miss Tremloe's guitar.

The rug she tripped over was a new one, which she hadn't seen before. It opened its mouth and grinned at her. It had a toothy grin.

"There, you see! *That's* my crocodile, Miss!" said Harriet.

THE HUNGRY CROCODILE

"I don't think it is your crocodile, Harriet," said Anthea. "It looks much too big."

"So would you, if you had been eating teachers," said Harriet.

"Go away! Go away, you nasty thing!" cried Miss Granston, and she hit the crocodile on the snout with the remains of Mr. Tiger's pipe.

"Oh, don't hurt him, Miss," said Harriet. "Poor Crocky!"

But Miss Granston was roused, and she attacked fiercely. "Go! Go! Go!" She plunged after the crocodile, which did a desperate zigzag round the Valor heater and disappeared up the ventilator shaft it had come by, leaving the well-chewed grid clanging behind it.

"I have saved my school!" cried Miss Granston dramatically.

"I think you've been awfully nasty to my crocodile," said Harriet.

"Your crocodile ate my Staff!" said Miss Granston. "They were good, kind teachers, with the Slow Street Primary Spirit! Well, some of them had it, anyway. I did not want to lose them. They were like my children, my own little children!"

"You should have stuck to snails, Harriet," said Anthea. "Snails don't eat teachers."

"Teachers are too big," said Harriet. "Snails only nibble little things. Crocodiles are much better!"

"I don't suppose your crocodile would eat children, do you, Harriet?" asked Anthea, nervously. Privately, she supposed it would, which was why she had been keeping out of the way, but she didn't want to say so in case Harriet was upset.

"Oh! Oh! My School! My Pupils!" shrieked Miss Granston, and she disappeared screaming into the corridor, where she broke the Fire Alarm Glass. "Evacuate the School At Once! There is a Teacher-Eating crocodile on the Prowl!"

"Harriet," said Anthea. "What's that?"

She was looking at the glass panel above the door of the Staff Toilet. Something was waving at her through it. It looked like a pair of feet, upside down, in tartan socks.

Beneath the tartan socks, were a pair of pale legs in tartan trousers, although only an inch or two of them showed.

"Mrs. Whitten, upside down," said Harriet, who was good at puzzles.

And she opened the door.

Mrs. Whitten fell out first, and all the other teachers fell out after her.

"You haven't been eaten at all, Mr. Tiger!" squealed Anthea in delight, skipping forward to greet him.

Harriet thought it was time to go, before one of the disheveled teachers connected her with the crocodile who hadn't eaten them.

"HARRIET!" said Mr. Tiger.

"Sir?"

Harriet stopped.

"Harriet, was that your crocodile?"

"Yes, Sir."

"You brought it to school?"

"Yes, Sir."

Miss Tremloe, Miss Ash, and Mrs. Barton leaped toward Harriet, intent on revenge.

"STOP!" commanded Mr. Tiger. "Control yourselves, ladies, please!" Then he stuck what was left of his pipe back in his mouth and tried puffing it, but it wouldn't puff, because the crocodile had spoiled the tobacco.

"Harriet," he said, severely. "Your crocodile has upset all these dear ladies and your Headmistress, who is at this moment evacuating the school. I feel it is your duty to retrieve your crocodile, and place it under restraint."

"All right, Sir," said Harriet.

"NOW, Harriet!" said Mr. Tiger.

6 | The Crocodile Hunt

"We have come for our crocodile," said the Zoo Superintendent.

"And about time too!" snapped Miss Granston, waving the School aspirin bottle in her hand. "What sort of Zoo are you, anyway?"

The entire school was lined up in the playground, class by class, with the teachers, or what was left of them. Miss Wilson was having hysterics, flat on her back in the hockey goal-net. Miss Ash was ashen. Miss Tremloe was trying to mend her guitar, and Mrs. Whitten, whose shoes had been eaten by the crocodile, was standing in her tartan knee socks trying to comfort Mrs. Barton, who seemed a broken woman.

The Zoo Superintendent and six keepers had arrived in a big yellow van, hastily summoned by Miss Granston. Now they were lined up in the playground with nets and stun-guns, ready to hunt the crocodile.

"Madam!" cried the Zoo Superintendent. "One of our crocodiles is missing! We demand the full cooperation of the General Public, and that means you."

"I am not the General Public," said Miss Granston coldly. "I am the Headmistress of Slow Street Primary School, I'll have you know, and your crocodile is trespassing on my premises."

"Our crocodile was stolen!" said the Superintendent.

"Borrowed," muttered Anthea, but nobody took any notice.

"Young man," said Miss Granston. "At this moment two members of my Staff and a Pupil are taking their lives in their hands, crocodile hunting on my premises, due to your failure to keep your crocodile under proper control. I shall report this matter to the appropriate authorities."

"We count the crocodiles twice a day," said the Zoo Superintendent.

"In that case," said Miss Granston. "You must allow me to lend you one of my P2s. Evidently some of your Staff are unable to count! The fact of the matter is that one of your crocodiles is on my premises. Pray have it removed!"

And she flounced away.

"Action Stations, men!" cried the Zoo Superintendent, and the Zoo keepers moved slowly toward the school, nets and stun-guns to the fore.

Meanwhile, in the school basement, Harriet was following a clue. Close behind her came Mr. Tiger, trying to stick together his pipe, and Mr. Cousins, who had past experience of crocodile hunts, up the Amazon.

"There's a clue," said Mr. Cousins, pointing to a smudge of white on the side of a trash bag.

"And another!" said Mr. Tiger, pointing in front of the first.

"Oh, do come on," cried Harriet, who had already disappeared over the top of a mountain of trash bags, hot on the trail of her crocodile.

Trailing this particular crocodile wasn't very difficult, for it had paused on its way through the school kitchens for a dip in the tapioca pudding, the nearest thing it had seen to a steaming jungle marsh all day. Now, as it waddled on, it left tapioca drips behind it.

Mr. Cousins and Mr. Tiger started up the pile of bags, following the tapioca. Mr. Cousins went first, because of his Amazonian experience, and Mr. Tiger came second, because he was too sensible to go first. Mr. Tiger had survived many dangers, including World War II and three years at school with Harriet, and he wasn't going to be caught by a crocodile.

Mr. Cousins reached the top of the pile of bags, and his flashlight flickered into the space below.

"Where is she?" said Mr. Tiger.

There was no sign of Harriet.

Mr. Cousins blanched.

"Eaten?" he gasped.

Harriet was HIS responsibility. A mere child. A child who, with her childish sense of humor, had somehow taken home a crocodile from a Zoo trip undertaken in HIS care. Mr. Cousins might be small and fat and old and almost bald, but he was brave, and he cared.

"No such luck," said Mr. Tiger, who knew Harriet better than that. If it came to a straight fight between Harriet and a crocodile, he felt sorry for the crocodile.

"But where is she, Tiger? Where is she?"

"Calm down," said Mr. Tiger philosophically. "Listen!"

They stood in silence at the foot of the mountain of trash bags in the school basement, listening.

The only sound was a faint and very distant whistling.

"Ah ha," said Mr. Cousins, not because it meant anything, but because it was something to say. He didn't know what the whistling was supposed to mean, but he didn't want to look stupid.

"There!" snapped Mr. Tiger, and he dropped to the ground, pressing his ear to the floor. Unfortunately, he didn't realize that the floor was covered in tapioca until he was down there.

"Euugh!" said Mr. Tiger.

"What's the matter?" said Mr. Cousins, nervously scratching his solitary hair.

"I've got tapioca in my ear," said Mr. Tiger.

"I see," said Mr. Cousins, wondering if the strain had been too much.

"LISTEN!" cried Mr. Tiger. "That whistling. It is coming from beneath us."

"Is it?" said Mr. Cousins.

"The drains!" cried Mr. Tiger. "Harriet has followed the crocodile into the drains!" And he bounded toward the raised manhole cover in the corner of the basement, where the last sludgy specks of tapioca betrayed what had taken place.

"Oh no! Poor child!" cried Mr. Cousins, wringing his hands. "Alone, in the drains, with a crocodile! She will surely be eaten!"

Meanwhile, down below in the darkness, Harriet went on, whistling as she went, feeling her way down into the drains beneath Slow Street. It was a bit smelly, but otherwise she didn't mind it. She was determined to catch up with her crocodile and reach it before the Zoo men, with their stun-guns.

Soon her eyes became accustomed to the dark, and she was able to pick her way along the deep tunnels, carefully following the tapioca marks.

But the marks grew fainter and fainter, until at last Harriet came to a place where several drains came together, joining one big channel. There were no tapioca marks to show where the crocodile had gone.

"Crocky? Crocky?" she called, but there was no answer, except the echo, *"Crocky Crocky,"* which rumbled down the tunnels.

Harriet stood still, unsure what to do next.

Go home?

Abandon her crocodile to the Zoo men

who would catch up with him and shoot him with their stun-guns?

Press on . . . on through miles and miles of what might be the wrong tunnel, while her crocodile waddled or swam in a different direction, depending on which route he had taken?

"What shall I do?" Harriet asked herself, and the echo from the four tunnels thundered back at her, "WHAT SHALL I DO?" over and over again, until she was nearly deafened.

Beneath the streets of Mitford a strange sound echoed and re-echoed, up and down the drains and sewers, through the cable pipes, along drains and ventilators and shafts and tunnels, through basements and railway tunnels.

The junction of the Slow Street tunnels was like a vast microphone, into which Harriet was whistling.

Far, far away, at Mitford Zoo, the whistling penetrated the crocodile cage.

One stirred, and then another.

It was the Call. The Call of the Wild. At least they thought it was. In fact it was Harriet's Snail Whistle.

The crocodiles came alive; they slithered and clambered around their cage, haunted by the sound.

At last one found a grating.

Three of them raised it, with a Triple Snout Lift.

One by one, lured by the echoed whistling from the depths, the crocodiles departed down the drains of Mitford, following the whistle.

Strange and enticing, it lured them on. The sound that had brought Harriet her first crocodile, greatly magnified by the echoing tunnels, drew all the rest irresistibly toward her.

Suddenly there was a lot of activity in the drains.

The Zoo Superintendent and his men had piled down the manhole cover, looking for Mr. Tiger and Mr. Cousins, who had gone down looking for Harriet, who had gone down looking for her crocodile, who

had got lost somewhere underneath Slow Street Primary.

They were all very busy looking for each other and meanwhile, from the direction of the Zoo, the rest of the crocodiles were on the slither.

7 | Lots of Crocodiles

"Harriet! Harriet!" Mr. Cousins called. He was wading along a drain with his trousers rolled up to the knees and his shoes tied by the laces around his neck.

"HARRIET!" boomed Mr. Tiger.

Their calls echoed back to them down the long dark dripping tunnels that led beneath the streets of Mitford.

"It's no use," said Mr. Cousins. "I give up. We can still hear the whistling, but where is it coming from?"

The trouble was that the whistling seemed to be coming from every direction at once, as the sound echoed up and down the tunnels.

"Let's go back," said Mr. Cousins.

It was then that Mr. Tiger gently pointed out that they didn't know where back *was*.

"Oh," said Mr. Cousins.

"Perhaps we could find a street grating, with a ladder leading up to it?" suggested Mr. Tiger.

"Haven't seen any, have you?" said Mr. Cousins, scratching at his single hair again. It was now damp, and rather the worse for wear.

"No," said Mr. Tiger. "No. I have to agree there. Indeed I do."

"We're lost!" exclaimed Mr. Cousins. "Lost in the drains!"

"Agreed," said Mr. Tiger.

"We may never escape!" said Mr. Cousins, tears welling in his eyes at the thought of a life spent in the drains of Mitford, searching for a whistling Harriet.

"Do not despair!" said Mr. Tiger, trying to sound cheerful and philosophical.

"Why not?" demanded Mr. Cousins.

There was a long silence, with only the sound of the water lapping round their knees and Harriet's distant whistling to disturb them.

"I don't know why not," said Mr. Tiger. "It just doesn't seem very helpful. Surely you must have been in stickier positions than this in the Amazon?"

"No," said Mr. Cousins in a sulky voice.

They waded on.

"I think we could . . . ," Mr. Cousins began, but Mr. Tiger waved his arms at him and said, "Shush! Listen! What's that?"

Mr. Cousins shushed and listened.

Then he looked.

Coming at them, through the darkness, were *eyes*, eyes that moved with a slithery slinky sound through the shallow water.

"Whatever can they be?" mused Mr. Tiger, peering into the darkness.

But Mr. Cousins, with the benefit of his Amazonian Experiences, *knew*.

"Crocodiles!" he screeched. "Crocodiles, Mr. Tiger! We are pursued by crocodiles!"

They splashed away and the dark, slinking-slurching eyes came after them, gleaming coldly at the prospect of the two man-sized dinners that had suddenly presented themselves.

Mr. Tiger and Mr. Cousins splashed and puffed and blew and stumbled on and, as they ran, the sound of Harriet's whistling grew fainter.

The crocodiles, sensing dinner, had forgotten the whistling. They were intent on a good meal.

"Quick! Quick!" breathed Mr. Cousins, tugging Mr. Tiger on. "Look, there is light ahead!"

"Euugh!" said Mr. Tiger, who seemed to have swallowed what was left of his pipe, and was trying to cough it up.

"On! On!" cried Mr. Cousins, pulling him forward.

They came to the foot of a long metal ladder, and were halfway up it when something bit the bottom rung.

C-r-e-a-k! The bottom of the ladder snapped away from the wall.

The two teachers climbed on, in a frenzy, aware that something was slithering and snapping up the rungs below them, as the ladder shook. Only just in time they reached the grill at the top and shoved it upward.

Mr. Tiger's head emerged in the school playground, beside the hockey net where Miss Wilson had just about got herself untangled.

She heard a sound and looked round. There was a head on the ground beside her.

"Aaaaaaaaahaaaaahhhh!" shrieked Miss Wilson. "Something has bitten off Mr. Tiger's head!"

"Nonsense!" barked Mr. Tiger, and then something *nibbled* his feet.

He shot out of the manhole, followed by Mr. Cousins.

"You brave men! You have saved us from the crocodiles!" cried Miss Granston, ever the optimist.

"Not *exactly*, I'm afraid," said Mr. Tiger, and the next moment a green snout emerged from the manhole.

And another.

And another.

And another.

And lots and lots of others, in fact nearly all the Zoo crocodiles came slopping out of the manhole, bar one or two who had got lost on the way through the Mitford drains.

Miss Ash climbed up on a car roof.

Miss Tremloe prepared to make a last stand, using her guitar as a weapon.

Mrs. Whitten fled.

Miss Granston, a born leader, took one look at the crocodiles and summoning up all the Slow Street Spirit, cried. "Charge!"

She charged, but nobody else did.

As she charged past, Mr. Tiger grabbed one arm and Mr. Cousins grabbed the other. They hooked her off her feet, and kept running in the opposite direction.

"We shall never retreat!" bawled Miss Granston. "What about the Slow Street Spirit?"

"What about it?" said Mr. Tiger, throwing her over the playground fence to a place of safety in a bramble bush.

Pupils and teachers were fleeing everywhere, as the crocodiles snapped on. Most of P6 got through the gate, and headed for home. Marky Owens caught his jacket on the fence, and almost got eaten. Sylvester Wise got on his bicycle with Rita Green and Hector Smith and Wally Thom, which were too much for the bicycle and too much for Sylvester.

"Miss Wilson!" cried Mr. Cousins, turning back toward the crocodile-infested playground.

Miss Wilson lay unconscious in the goal net, with the crocodiles milling around, deciding which bit to bite off first.

The biggest one made his choice, opened his mouth, and was preparing to bite when, at the very last moment, a brave figure emerged from the manhole, whistling.

"Harriet!" cried Anthea. "Harriet to the Rescue!"

8 | Harriet to the Rescue!

The cruel crocodile jaws hung open just in front of Miss Wilson.

The crocodile's eyes gleamed.

At the Zoo, it would have been just about dinnertime.

Then . . .

. . . a sweet familiar sound.

The crocodile faltered, and turned away.

They were all turning away, following Harriet, who was picking her way across the playground, clutching her own special little crocodile, which she had found in the deepest drain beneath the streets of Mitford.

"Open the gate!" commanded Mr. Tiger.

Harriet marched through, while every-body else hid, and Miss Granston went looking for the Zoo men. But that was no good, for they were lost beneath the streets of Mitford.

"Well done, Harriet!" called Anthea, from a safe distance, as Harriet led the croc-odiles up the road away from the school.

Doors slammed.

Crocodiles nipped in and out of gardens, eating plastic gnomes and trampling on rose beds. Milk bottles were smashed. Postmen clambered on top of mailboxes and old ladies climbed trees. One of the crocodiles bit a bus.

On and on they went through the streets of Mitford, back to the Zoo, following the whistle. By the time they were all inside and safe in their cage, Harriet was quite out of breath.

She sat down on the steps of the Zoo and waited for help to arrive.

Moments later Mr. Tiger drove up, with Miss Granston and Anthea in the back seat.

"Well done, Harriet," said Miss Granston. "That was splendid. You showed the Slow Street Spirit."

"Super whistling, Harriet," said Anthea. "Good Show!" said Mr. Tiger.

They all went back to Slow Street, where Harriet was awarded a Gold Medal by the Crocodile Preservation Society and presented with Life Membership of the Zoo, but it wasn't a happy Harriet who eventually found her way back to the P7 Classroom and sat at her desk, fingering the chewed end of crocodile rope.

She blew a bubble and thought about her little crocodile. Mr. Tiger was right, of course; it would be happier at home with its mother, and anyway Harriet couldn't afford to feed it on her pocket money, even if she gave it all her school dinners.

Still . . .

Harriet started whistling, softly.

"Harriet?" Anthea's head appeared around the doorway, and then the rest of her stepped inside. "Harriet, DON'T DO THAT!" And Anthea took a quick look around, to make sure that no crocodiles were creeping up on her.

"I was whistling very softly," said Harriet.

"Something might hear you all the same," said Anthea.

"Nothing will," said Harriet sadly.

But something had.

Actually it had heard Harriet a long time before, when she first came back to school after having the flu but it wasn't very quick-moving, and so it had only just managed to arrive.

It was the Yellow Snail, World Champion of Slow Street Primary School, and it came slithering round the side of Harriet's inkwell to greet her.

"Look, Harriet!" gasped Anthea.

"MY SNAIL!" cried Harriet.

The snail wagged its tiny horns at her.

"No more crocodiles," said Anthea happily. She didn't like snails very much, but she could live with them, if they made Harriet happy.

"Let's go home," said Harriet.

"We'll have a Harriet-the-Heroine Party of sausages-on-sticks and ham sandwiches and strawberries and jelly and ice cream, with dried-up lettuce leafs for the Yellow Snail," said Anthea.

They went out into Slow Street.

"Oh, look!" said Harriet, stopping in her tracks.

"What is it?" said Anthea.

"It's a digger," said Harriet. "You dig up streets with it. You can move great big things. You could . . ."

"No, Harriet," said Anthea.

But Harriet didn't hear her. Harriet was already in the driver's seat.

About the Author

Martin Waddell was born in Belfast and educated in Northern Ireland. Through the Ulster Arts Council he has encouraged, promoted, and assisted children's writing in schools, showing children how authors write their books and how children themselves can build a story. He is the author of more than twenty books for children, including *Harriet and the Haunted School*.